SOMETHING
NOBLE

SOMETHING
NOBLE

WILLIAM KOWALSKI

RAVEN BOOKS
an imprint of
ORCA BOOK PUBLISHERS

Library and Archives Canada Cataloguing in Publication

Kowalski, William, 1970-
Something noble / William Kowalski.
(Rapid reads)

Issued also in electronic formats.
ISBN 978-1-4598-0013-7

I. Title. II. Series: Rapid reads
ps8571.o985S65 2012   c813'.54   c2011-907748-5

First published in the United States, 2012
Library of Congress Control Number: 2011943697

Summary: In order to save her son's life, a single mom must
try to convince a selfish drug dealer to donate one of his kidneys
to his half brother. (RL 3.0)

MIX
Paper from
responsible sources
FSC® C016245
www.fsc.org

*Orca Book Publishers is dedicated to preserving the environment and has
printed this book on paper certified by the Forest Stewardship Council®.*

Orca Book Publishers gratefully acknowledges the support for
its publishing programs provided by the following agencies:
the Government of Canada through the Canada Book Fund and the
Canada Council for the Arts, and the Province of British Columbia
through the BC Arts Council and the Book Publishing Tax Credit.

Design by Teresa Bubela
Cover photography by Getty Images

ORCA BOOK PUBLISHERS
PO Box 5626, Stn. B
Victoria, BC Canada
V8R 6S4

ORCA BOOK PUBLISHERS
PO Box 468
Custer, WA USA
98240-0468

www.orcabook.com
Printed and bound in Canada.

15 14 13 12 • 4 3 2 1

To all those who need a second chance

CHAPTER ONE

I just want to tell you straight up that this story has no happy ending.

But it doesn't have a sad ending either. It's a story about being a mom, so it has a lot of happy and sad in it. Like motherhood itself, it has no ending at all.

That's because you never stop being a mom. You don't stop when your kids go to sleep at night. You don't stop when they grow up and move away. Being a mom is not just a job. It's an identity. Maybe you already know what I'm talking about.

If not, you will by the time you're done hearing my story.

My life has never been boring. I'm not an important or exciting person, but sometimes some pretty wild things happen to me. Usually they don't come right on top of each other like this though.

This is the story of one remarkable year that was full of one wild thing after another. It was a year that changed my life and the lives of everyone I cared about. And it starts in my least favorite place of all: a doctor's office.

Let me take you back to that doctor's office right now.

* * *

My son, Dre, is sixteen years old. He's been feeling sick for a while. We've been having a lot of tests done. Now we're sitting and waiting for the doctor to come talk to us.

Dre feels too sick to be nervous, so I'm nervous for both of us. He lies on the exam table with his arm over his eyes. He's so tall that his feet hang way down off the end of the table. I still can't believe how big my baby is. I carried him on my hip for so long sometimes I can still feel him there. Now look at him. He's a giant with dreadlocks. So handsome the girls can't take their eyes off him.

I was only sixteen myself when I had Dre. I try to imagine him becoming a father at this age. It's a horrible thought. I didn't know a damn thing when I was sixteen. For the millionth time, I think about how amazing it is that we even survived. I was so stupid when I was that age. So young and stupid.

But here we are. We made it through a lot of bad times. Only now my baby is sick, and I have this horrible feeling that more bad times are around the corner.

When I get nervous, I talk. So I keep on chattering away to Dre, even though he isn't answering me.

After a while he says, "Mama, give it a rest. I'm too sick for small talk."

So we sit and wait in silence.

Finally the door opens. A new doctor walks in. He stops and looks at Dre, then at me. Then he looks at his chart, like he's making sure he has the right people. We get that a lot. That's what it's like when your kid's skin is a different color from yours. I guess people wonder if you're just borrowing him or something.

"Señora Gonzalez," says the doctor. "*Buenos días. Me llamo* Doctor Wendell."

I get that a lot too. People think I don't speak English just because I look Latina. I don't even get mad anymore. I don't have the energy.

"Hi," I say. "How you doing, Doctor Wendell."

"Fine," says the doctor, without missing a beat. And I realize he wasn't being rude. We live in a big city. He must meet a lot of people who don't speak English. So maybe he's not so bad after all. He closes the door.

"Let's talk about Dre," he says. He pronounces it *Dree*.

"It's pronounced *Dray*," I say.

"Sorry," says the doctor. "I know you weren't expecting to meet a new doctor today. So let me tell you about myself. I'm a kidney specialist. I was called in because of the results of Dre's tests. I think the reason Dre feels so sick all the time is because he might have kidney problems."

I nod. I knew it was going to be something serious.

"What kind of problems?" I ask.

"Well, the job of your kidneys is to clean the impurities out of your blood. If they can't do that, your blood gets dirtier and dirtier. It's like you're being poisoned.

5

So what's going on here is that Dre's kidneys need some help doing their job."

Dr. Wendell puts down the clipboard and waits for me to talk. It used to be that doctors never had time for us. We were just one more poor family of color. I used to hate it. It made me feel like our lives were unimportant to them. But now they are spending more and more time with us. They look at us in a new way now. And even though it sounds crazy, I hate this even more. It shows how serious Dre's case is. I almost miss the days when we weren't worth paying attention to. At least then nothing was really wrong.

I look at Dre. He hasn't moved. I grab his toe and wiggle his foot.

"Well, baby," I say, "at least now we know what the problem is."

"Mmm," says Dre. That's the sound he always makes when he's sick. I can tell he feels horrible.

"Is it one kidney or both?" I ask.

"I'll need to run some more tests to be sure," says Dr. Wendell. "The nurse will take your blood, Dre."

"Mmm," says Dre again. He's so sick he doesn't even complain about one more needle. The nurse comes in again and draws another vial of blood. Dr. Wendell promises to call us as soon as he gets the results. Then I help Dre out to the car, and we head home.

"What time is it?" he asks.

"Three o'clock," I say. "Why?"

"Because I gotta go do my paper routes."

"Uh-uh," I say. "No way. You're gonna have to give those up. The doctor said you gotta rest."

"But, Mama," says Dre. "What about the money?"

Dre makes about three hundred bucks a month from his two paper routes.

It might not sound like much, but it makes a big difference to us. Yet our neighborhood is getting worse and worse. I won't be sorry to see him stop walking the streets by himself.

I got mugged last year right in front of my own house. Broad daylight. He pointed a knife at me and everything. I didn't get hurt, but I was scared to death. And he took the twenty bucks I had on me. That was twenty bucks I could not afford to lose.

I would move to a safer neighborhood, but moving costs money. Right now I'm just keeping it together financially. I'm mostly unemployed. I only have one job, as opposed to my usual three or four. We have enough to eat and pay the rent. But I'm just one flat tire or one speeding ticket away from being bankrupt. And the house is mine. I'm not giving it up just because punks have taken over the east side of the city. They'll have to kill me first.

"Forget about the money," I say. "We'll figure something out."

"But what?" Dre says.

"I dunno," I say. "You're too young to worry about these things."

"No, I'm not," he says. "You were my age when you had me."

"Let me worry about money. That's my job. You just take care of yourself. That's all that matters."

"I'm not all that matters. There's Marco too," says Dre quietly.

I love him for saying that. I look out the window so he doesn't see me crying.

CHAPTER TWO

Our house is a tiny bungalow. It's on a side street just off one of the busiest avenues in the city. The front yard is a postage stamp. The porch roof is about as big as a child's umbrella, and about as good at keeping you dry when you're fumbling for your keys in the rain. Inside, there is just a living room, a kitchen, two bedrooms and a bathroom. Each room is about the size of a phone booth. But it's mine, dammit. I bought it with my own money, back when things were better. And you better believe I keep it clean. My boys both knew how to make their own beds by the time they were five years old. And if you use a plate or a fork, you wash it. Just because we're poor doesn't mean we have to live in filth. You can be poor and clean at the same time.

Marco, my other son, is six years old. He's taking a nap on the couch. His digital camera is on a cord around his neck. Marco loves to take pictures of anything and everything. My dream for him is that someday he'll work for *National Geographic*.

Ernest, his dad, is waiting for me. Ernest's parents are both from China, which means Marco is half Chinese, a quarter Latino, and a quarter white. The white comes from my dad, the Latino from my mom. Dre's father was black, so Dre is African, European and Latino. When we're all together, the house looks like the lobby of the United Nations.

"You let him sleep with this thing on?" I say. "He'll strangle to death." I take the camera off Marco's neck.

"That's an old wives' tale," says Ernest. "If he started choking, he'd wake up. Besides, I tried to take it off him and he wouldn't let me."

"Sometimes those old wives were right," I say.

Ernest is wearing the kind of clothes I hate on him: a tight muscle shirt and jeans that show off how much he's been going to the gym. He never worked out once during the years we were married. Sometimes I wonder if he's trying to get me back, making me jealous by showing off his new body. It ain't working.

I keep him waiting while I go with Dre to his room and help him take off his shoes. I make him lie down to rest. Then I go back out into the living room.

"What's going on?" Ernest asks me. He crosses his arms and waits. Ernest is mostly bald, and when he's concerned, he doesn't just wrinkle his forehead. He wrinkles his whole scalp.

I fill him in. He nods.

"Well, you just let me know if there's anything I can do, baby," he says. "Anything at all, I'm there for you."

I hate it when he calls me baby. That's another thing he never did when we were married. I would like nothing better than for him to just go away and leave me alone. But we have a son together, and I need his support.

And at least Ernest isn't in jail, which is more than I can say for some people's fathers. Ernest has a decent job, and he believes in taking care of his kid.

"I'll need you to help with Marco," I say. "And I hate leaving Dre alone while he's this sick. I know he's not your kid, but if you're here with Marco anyway, it doesn't matter, right?"

Ernest nods.

"No problem," he says. "Dre is a great kid. We always got along well."

"I have to go to work now," I say. "Can you stay with them until I get back?"

"Sure thing, baby," says Ernest. He starts moving in closer, for what reason I am afraid to ask, so I dodge him and go into the bathroom. It's going to take a lot more than this to make up for what he did. But I don't even want to think about that right now. I need to start getting ready for work.

I'm trained as a continuing care assistant. I go into people's homes and do some nursing and some light housekeeping as they recover from illnesses. Or sometimes I just sit with them while they die. I feel like it's important work. So do my clients. The only ones who don't seem to feel that way are the ones who sign my paycheck. When the work is steady, it's not a bad living. It's enough to pay the bills. But it hasn't been steady for a long time. This economy is destroying us.

I could drive to work. But I decide to leave my car at home to save gas money. I take the bus a few miles down the road to a senior citizen's apartment complex. This is where I'm working right now. I let myself into the apartment and call out:

"Miss Emily! It's Linda Gonzalez."

I don't hear anything, but I wasn't expecting to. I go into the bedroom. Miss Emily is asleep. She's a very old, very tiny woman who is dying of cancer. She doesn't have long left. I stroke her hand lightly. She gives a little moan.

"It's Linda, Miss Emily," I say again. "You need anything?"

Miss Emily is well cared for. She's one of the lucky ones. A lot of poor people die alone, in what you might call undignified circumstances. That means lying in their own filth in the middle of a public hospital ward. Not Miss Emily. I guess she saved enough money in her working life so she could afford to die in private. Kind of depressing when you look at it that way. Isn't there more to life than that? Working until you get old and die? Sometimes my life feels like that's all it is. It's my kids that make it all worthwhile.

Miss Emily wakes up enough to press her morphine drip. The pain must be pretty bad. I read her chart. The visiting nurse hasn't left much in the way of orders. She knows the end is near. Right now we're just keeping her comfortable. I pull back the sheets from her feet and look at her toes. They're starting to curl. That's always a sign that the end is coming. You won't find that in any textbook. It's just a trick I picked up from nurses who have been on the job a long time. We know a lot of things they don't teach you in medical school.

There's not much for me to do. The place is pretty clean. There are no dishes in the sink, no meals to be made. So I sit down next to Miss Emily's bed and pick up the book that's sitting on the floor. The title is *The Audacity of Hope* by Barack Obama.

"Let's see," I say. "Where did we leave off?"

I read about when Mr. Obama's mother was dying. It's funny to think that the president of the United States of America is just as powerless against cancer as the rest of us.

It doesn't matter what the words are. Miss Emily probably doesn't understand me anyway. But I know she can hear the sound of my voice, and she finds it comforting.

Suddenly I feel my cell phone go off. I have it set to vibrate. I stop reading and go into the other room.

"Hello?"

"It's Ernest. You gotta go to the hospital."

CHAPTER THREE

I've got that feeling every mother dreads. Which one of my boys is it? Please, God, nothing serious, okay? I can't deal with another thing right now. I'm too tired.

"Why? What happened?"

"It's Dre. He collapsed. I called nine-one-one. They took him away in an ambulance."

"Okay," I say, as calmly as possible. "Can you stay with Marco?"

"I'll take him home with me," says Ernest. "He can spend the night at my place."

I hang up on Ernest and call my head office. I explain the situation to them, hoping they will let me leave early. They say it all depends on if I can get someone to replace me. Which really means it's my problem, not theirs.

I call the girl who was supposed to come on next and ask if she can come in a few hours early. She says she wasn't planning on it. So I'm reduced to begging her. My son is in the hospital, I say. Please. Just this once. I'll make it up to you somehow.

She agrees, but I will owe her. I don't care. I would mortgage my soul to help my kid. I wait until she shows up. Then I leave for the hospital, riding the slowest bus on the planet. After what feels like ten lifetimes, I finally make it to my son's bedside. He's in a little room in the ER.

I promised myself a long time ago I wouldn't shed any more tears in front of my children. But when I see his face, looking scared and exhausted, it's all I can do to keep it together.

"Hey, bunny boy," I say. That was my nickname for him when he was a baby. Normally he would yell at me for using it. How I wish he was healthy enough to be embarrassed.

"Mama," he says.

"Listen, you hang in there," I say. "We're gonna get you fixed up."

Dre doesn't answer. But I gotta keep talking. This is one of those times when silence is not golden.

"You remember back in the old days, when it was just you and me against the world? We made it through some rough times, kiddo. But we kept each other going. I was there for you, and you were there for me. You're my whole life, Dre. So just you remember that. A little old kidney ain't nothing."

"I don't wanna die," Dre whispers.

"You're not gonna die. You're gonna live. Hear me? Don't let me hear that word again."

"Okay," Dre whispers.

"Let me hear you say it. You're gonna live."

"Gonna live," Dre says. He can barely get the words out.

Dr. Wendell shows up a few minutes later along with a couple of nurses. I'm so grateful to see him. He feels like the only friend I've got.

"Things are worse than we realized," he says.

"What's going on?" I ask.

"I got Dre's results back, but I didn't have a chance to call you yet. Both of Dre's kidneys are having problems. He needs dialysis right away. They're going to take him down now and put in a shunt. That's like a needle that never comes out. After that you can sit with him if you want. The treatment takes a while."

I start to follow them out of the room. But Dr. Wendell puts his hand on my shoulder.

"Wait," he says. "I need to talk to you a minute."

"What is it?" I ask. I watch Dre's bed disappear down the hall.

"It's about the future," he says. "I'm afraid the dialysis is only a temporary fix."

"What do you mean?"

"My tests showed that both his kidneys are malfunctioning. Dre is going to need a transplant as soon as possible," says Dr. Wendell.

I stare at him. "You mean...a whole new kidney?"

"That's right," he says.

For a moment I feel like I'm going to faint. First I wonder how Dre is going to deal with this news. And then all I can think of is how much this is going to cost. I barely afford to pay the phone bill.

But then I remember not to worry about that kind of stuff. The important thing is Dre. Money is temporary. Love is forever.

"Wow," I say. "This is just—"

"Overwhelming," says the doctor. "I know."

"So how do we get a new kidney?" I ask.

"Basically, we have to wait for a donor," says the doctor. "There's a waiting list. You're already on it."

"You mean we have to wait for someone to die so Dre can have his kidney," I say.

I don't even want to ask how long that can take. It feels like the wrong question. Our family's happiness depends on some other family's misery. It seems cruel and unfair. What kind of a world is this anyway? Sometimes I don't want any part of it.

"There's another way. Someone could donate a kidney," says Dr. Wendell.

I have the solution before I've finished drawing my next breath. I'll give Dre one of my own kidneys. Hell, I would give him my life if I had to. But Dr. Wendell can tell what I'm thinking.

"We can't use one of yours," he says. "You can't be a donor for Dre."

"What? Why not?"

"Dre has a very rare blood type," he explains. "It's AB negative."

"I remember," I say. They told me that when he was a baby. I thought it was strange he wasn't the same blood type as his mama, but they said that happens all the time. "So what?"

"It would be best if the kidney came from someone with the same blood type," says Dr. Wendell. "And it would be best of all if that person was a relative. That way, the kidney stands the best chance of being accepted by Dre's body. If it works, he could have a long, healthy life."

"And if it doesn't?"

"I don't want to sugarcoat it for you, Linda, so I'm going to tell you straight up," says Dr. Wendell. "If Dre's body rejects the kidney, he'll stay very sick, and he'll probably get sicker. We'll have to do another transplant, which will be hard on him. His immune system is already weak. I'm sorry to tell you this, but you need all the facts. There's a chance he could die."

I reach out for the wall. I need something to hold me up.

"So the question I have to ask you is this," says Dr. Wendell. "What relatives does Dre have who have the same blood type and who might be willing to give him a kidney?"

CHAPTER FOUR

The search for the answer to that question takes me somewhere I never thought I would go: prison.

When I was young and stupid, I used to run with whoever made my mama maddest. In those days, that meant a young black boy who was always in trouble with the cops. His name was Terrell. He was lean and handsome, and he always did whatever he wanted. I thought he was a hero, because nobody could tell him what to do. My mama said to watch out, because I couldn't rely on him.

She predicted he would end up in prison. If he got me pregnant, she warned me, I wouldn't be able to depend on him. I didn't pay any attention to her. I thought it would be Terrell and me forever.

Guess what? Terrell knocked me up. He was the first boy I was ever with. Ten minutes of fun for sixteen years of consequences. When I told him there was a baby coming, he dumped me. Then he started spending more time in prison than out. I was a teenager with a baby and no high school diploma. If it wasn't for my mama, we would have been on the street. And Terrell wouldn't even have cared.

That's why I never visit Terrell. He and I have nothing to do with each other. But that's not my choice, it's his. He's still Dre's father. He could at least send Dre a birthday card if he wanted to. But he doesn't even bother. I don't think he would know Dre if he passed him on the street, even though they both have the same sloping shoulders, the same easy smile.

So if Terrell won't give Dre the time of day, why am I crazy enough to think he's going to give him a kidney?

Because I have no other choice.

* * *

Visiting hours at the prison is the most depressing thing I've ever seen. There are lots of families that remind me of myself when I was younger. Young women with small children, sometimes two or three, visiting their men in the big house. What kind of memories will these kids have when they're grown? How long before they're slinging drugs on a corner or sitting behind bars themselves?

I sit at the table, waiting for the guard to call Terrell's name. Finally the door opens and in he comes. He's changed a lot. He used to be cool and slick. Now he just looks like a shifty con. He's the kind of guy you cross the street to get away from. The kind of guy who thinks prison is a career. I can't believe I ever slept with someone like that. For the millionth time, I wish I could have a do-over. But then I wouldn't have Dre.

Terrell looks around. I can tell he wasn't expecting a visitor. He's surprised anyone wants to see him at all. I wonder when was the last time that someone came. He spots me, and the look on his face changes to shock. Then he recovers his sense of cool. He comes shuffling over and sits down.

"Hey, baby," he says. "How you doing?"

Just once, why couldn't I get called baby by someone I want to hear it from?

"Hey, Terrell," I say. "Long time no see."

"Yeah, no doubt," he says. "Damn, girl, your face takes me back. You miss me or somethin'?"

"Not hardly," I say.

"What are you doing here? I ain't seen you in years."

"It's about Dre," I say. "Our son."

Terrell looks confused for a moment. Like he doesn't even remember Dre exists. Then he nods.

"You got any cigarettes?" he asks.

I was ready for this. I remembered a friend of mine telling me that in prison cigarettes are like cash. She had a brother in the slammer, and he was always bugging her for smokes. So I brought Terrell a couple of packs. I didn't think it was a great idea to put that poison in his body if he was going to give my son a kidney, but then I figured he'd been smoking right along anyway. A couple more packs wasn't going to change anything.

I give Terrell the cigarettes. He nods in appreciation and lights one up.

"Dre in trouble?"

"You could say that."

"Just like his old man."

"No, he ain't." I say that a little too fast. I don't want to make him mad. But old hurts die hard.

"What's up?"

I don't beat around the bush. I tell him straight out. Terrell listens without changing his expression. Then he's quiet for a minute while he thinks.

"I got this rare blood type?" he asks.

"Yeah, you do," I say. "I remember these things."

"Okay," he says.

"Okay what?"

"Okay, I'll do it."

I'm so amazed I nearly fall off my seat.

"Just like that?" I say. "No bargaining? No excuses? No trying to get out of it?"

"Hell, no. I ain't like that no more," says Terrell. "This my boy we're talking about. Right?"

"Well, it's about time you thought of him as your son," I say.

"Besides," Terrell goes on, "I heard about something like this. This one dude, he gave his brother a kidney. It got him out of the joint early. You score a lotta points with the parole board for somethin' like that."

"You mean—?"

"I got another ten years in here," says Terrell. "I'm buggin'. I can't deal with it. My whole life is passin' me by. Next month we all have to quit smoking. I'd give someone my head if it would get me out early. You tell my boy he can have my kidney. He can have both kidneys and my liver too. Just as long as it gets my ass outta here."

CHAPTER FIVE

After my visit to Terrell, I feel two different ways. I'm happy Dre is going to get a kidney. But I can't believe Terrell's main concern is for himself. He really feels nothing for his own son. How can that be?

I guess it must be different for men. Dre didn't come out of his body. And he didn't watch him grow up. If he did, he would see him as a person. Not just a way of getting out of prison early.

I decide to call the parole board and ask if it's really true he can get out early for donating a kidney. They tell me there are no guarantees, but it would help Terrell's case a lot. It would show he's ready to start giving back to the world, instead of stealing from it. The way Terrell's mind works has me spinning. He had this whole angle figured in two seconds. Dre is just a means to an end.

It doesn't matter. It's not like we will owe him anything. We'll both be getting something out of the deal.

So I decide not to think about it anymore. And I also decide I'm not going to say anything to Dre about Terrell's real reason for wanting to help. He doesn't need to know. Let him think he has a father who cares. Let him feel for once like the world isn't a completely cold and hard place.

Dr. Wendell warned me that donating a kidney was complicated. Once we found a potential donor, he would have to do more tests to make sure it really was a good match. So I don't tell Dre yet that we might have a kidney for him. He doesn't even know I went to see his father. I let the doctor's office know Terrell said yes. They say they will start the process, whatever that means. We have to sit tight and wait. It shouldn't take too long.

In the meantime I take Dre every other day for dialysis. It helps him feel a lot better. There's no way he can go to school, so I get his homework for him. Last thing I want is for him to fall behind.

We have a lot of time to sit and talk while he's getting his treatments.

"You still thinking about college?" I ask him.

"Yeah," he says. "I'm still thinking about it."

"You keep those grades up, maybe you'll get a scholarship," I say.

"Yeah, well, we both know that's the only way I'm getting an education," he says.

"There's always the community college. You could start there. Learn some kind of a trade. Then move on up the ladder. Nothing wrong with that."

But Dre shakes his head. His dreadlocks whip back and forth.

"University," he says. "That's where I belong."

Dre sees himself as a professor. I don't know where he gets this from. I never liked school much. I certainly never thought about getting a higher education. I was happy just to finally get my GED when I was twenty-six, after almost ten years of being a single mom.

That was also the year I met Ernest and we got married. For a while, things were looking up. Ernest had a good job managing an electronics store. We lived in my little house. Soon Marco came along. We were a real family.

But Ernest had a little problem staying faithful. I don't know for sure how long his affair with that salesgirl was going on. I know one thing: I couldn't ever trust him again, not after she started calling our house. He swore up and down it would never happen again, but by then it was too late.

I can be a very understanding person… sometimes. If you break your promise to have your pizza at my house in thirty minutes or less, I'll give you a second chance. But if you break your marriage vows to me, you're out the door.

"I'm proud of you," I say to Dre.

"Why?"

"For going to university."

"Mama," he says, "what are you talking about? I haven't even finished high school yet."

"Yeah, I know," I say. "I'm just proud of you for even wanting to do it. You don't know how much that means to me. All a mother wants is for her kids to do well. And you will."

"If I make it through this, you mean," he says, nodding at the machine.

"You will," I say again. "I just know it."

Then the bad news comes. A few days later, I get a message on my cell to call Dr. Wendell's office.

"I'm afraid I have bad news," he says. "Terrell can't be a donor. There's no way."

My heart falls into my feet. I should have known this would happen.

"Why not?" I ask.

"We ask our potentials a list of questions," he says. "And one of those questions is, Have you ever done intravenous drugs?"

"Let me guess," I say. "He answered yes."

"I suppose we should be grateful he told the truth," says Dr. Wendell. "If he had any diseases, we would have caught them in the screening. But maybe something else would have popped up down the line, after it was too late. We can't take that chance."

"Does Terrell know?" I ask. I wonder how upset he is, now that he's not getting out of prison early.

"He knows. The nurse stopped the interview right there."

I go quiet. I'm just thinking.

"Linda," says Dr. Wendell. "Are you there?"

"I'm here."

"I realize this isn't good news. But there's another possibility. Terrell told me he has another son."

I can hardly believe my ears. But I don't know why I'm surprised either. Terrell probably has a whole tribe of kids out there, all from different mothers.

"And this person is listed as a potential donor for Terrell in case he ever needs blood," Dr. Wendell goes on.

"So he's the same blood type?"

"Yes. AB negative. And he'd be a close enough relative of Dre's. It could work."

"How do I find this person?"

"Terrell doesn't know where he is. I gather he hasn't had much contact with him. But he told me the name of his mother. She would know."

"Did he give you a phone number?"

"He doesn't have it," says Dr. Wendell. "It sounds like she's moved around a lot. And she and Terrell are not exactly on good terms."

I can certainly understand that.

"Well, how am I going to find her then?" I say, disappointed.

"Her last known address was here in the city," says Dr. Wendell. "And these days, with the Internet, you can find almost anyone pretty quickly."

"So if I get ahold of this woman, she could tell me where Terrell's other son is?"

"Possibly. It's worth a shot, don't you think?"

CHAPTER SIX

I have exactly two facts to go on: Terrell's other son is named LeVon, and his mother's name is Angelique Johnson. That's it. Armed with this tiny bit of information, I go to the library to use one of their computers. I don't have one of my own yet. That's top of the list of things to buy, if and when I ever get a full-time job.

Bringing up Google is easy. But then I'm stuck. Is it really just as simple as typing in their names? I try that, but nothing comes up that makes any sense. I take away LeVon's name and just use Angelique Johnson.

Again, a whole bunch of returns. But I'm getting closer. Some of them are directory listings. A lot of phone numbers and addresses. I just have to find the right one.

Then I realize I know more than I think I did. I know roughly how old she is. And I know she lives here in the city. Using this information, I get a directory listing. It turns out there is only one person named Angelique Johnson in this whole city. That doesn't mean it's her for sure. But it will be easy to find out.

I decide to go visit her in person. It would be too easy for her to hang up on me. I want to talk mother to mother. I have no idea what I'm going to say. I haven't got any kind of speech planned. I'm hoping it will just come out somehow.

Angelique Johnson lives not far from me, in the same part of the city. The poor part. The east side. She even lives in a house instead of an apartment.

But I can tell she doesn't own it. Her place is a lot more run-down than mine. There's trash in the yard. The weeds are taking over. The place needs a paint job. Empty bottles on the porch. I even see broken crack pipes in the street outside. This does not bode well. Angelique Johnson is the kind of person who gives the rest of us poor people a bad name.

It's about three o'clock in the afternoon. I knock on the door. It's locked tight, although around here that doesn't mean a person is away. People barricade themselves against crackheads and stray bullets.

I knock several times, but there's no answer at first. I was ready for that too. She probably thinks I'm a cop.

"Who is it?" a voice finally says from inside.

"Miz Johnson, my name is Linda Gonzalez. Can I talk to you?"

"What you want?"

"I need to talk to you about Terrell Jones."

"Terrell? The hell with Terrell!"

"I agree," I say. "Miz Johnson, I need your help bad. Can I please talk to you a minute? I have to ask you something about your boy LeVon."

For a while I don't hear anything. Then the door opens. She stands before me, a tiny black woman with frazzled hair. She doesn't look too good. She's some kind of user, I think. Maybe not the hard stuff. Maybe just booze. But she's not holding down a nine-to-five, that's for sure. She's blinking like she hasn't seen daylight in a while.

"What you wanna know about LeVon?" she demands.

"I need to find him," I say. "Terrell and I had a child together sixteen years ago. His name is Dre."

"If you woulda come to me first, I woulda told you stay away from Terrell Jones," Angelique announces. She puts one hand on her hip, and her head starts bopping side to side. "That fool ain't nothin' but trouble."

"I know that," I say. "Here's the thing. My son needs blood. And he has a rare blood type. Same kind your son has." I just told my first lie in years. It doesn't feel great. But it's only a little one. And Angelique isn't really listening to me anyway. She's the kind of person who only cares about her own problems.

"Yeah? You need to find LeVon? Good luck. Only time I ever see that boy is when he wants money. He ain't been around lately 'cause I got none to give him. As you can see." She spreads her arms out, as if to show me her entire life. I look past her into the house. It's a mess. There's hardly any furniture. Just a bunch of trash. And lots more empty bottles.

"How old is your son?" I ask.

"He's eighteen. No, wait, he's nineteen now."

That means Terrell already had a son when he met me. I never knew that, of course. He didn't say a word.

"Terrell never told me about you," I say.

"Where he at? He owes me child support."

I tell her where Terrell is at. "Good luck getting it," I add. "He never paid me a dime either."

Angelique stares me up and down. For a moment I think she's going to get hostile. I'm her rival in getting child support from Terrell. But then her expression changes.

"What do I care? Ain't neither of us ever gonna see a dime from that deadbeat," she says.

"Yeah, you're right there," I say. "Some guys oughta just be kept away from women."

"I'll tell you where LeVon hangs," she says. "Go down to the projects here. The one with the big fountain out in front that don't run anymore. You see a bunch of punks hanging around, one of them is LeVon. That's where he is every day."

I know exactly where she's talking about. It's one of the most notorious places in the city. Shootings, stabbings, drug deals, you name it. It all goes down at the Fountain.

Normally it's the kind of place I would steer away from. But if Dre's life depends on it, I'm going in, full steam ahead.

"What's he look like?"

"Tall like Terrell. Face just like him too. You know Terrell, you'll know LeVon."

"Thank you, Angelique," I say. And as I turn to leave, I add, "Good luck." Because I think she needs it even more than I do.

"Hey," she croaks as I'm walking away.

I turn again. I already know what she's going to ask.

"You think you could help a sister out? I'm in a bad way. Look at me." She stares at me with a zombie's eyes. She's holding her hand out, and it's trembling. "Terrell left me high and dry," she says.

Yeah, nineteen years ago, I want to say. *What have you done for yourself since then?*

Instead I reach into my purse and give her my last five dollars. I seriously cannot afford to do this. And I know she's just going to drink it. But I feel like I owe her something.

She snatches the money out of my hand and sticks it inside her bra. She doesn't even say thank you. She just scuttles back into the house like a crab into its shell, and the door slams shut.

CHAPTER SEVEN

Every big city has housing projects like ours. It's where they stick the people who can't afford to live anywhere. Everyone here is getting money from the government somehow. Welfare, food stamps, rent subsidy, something.

All these safety nets are a good thing. But they were never meant to keep people going forever. They're just supposed to use them until they can stand on their own. Yet poverty is a state of mind. And that's the hardest thing of all to change.

I know, because I grew up in a place just like this. And I was on welfare until I was twenty-six years old.

The big fountain Angelique was talking about is still dry. The city put it in a while ago to give the kids a place to cool off in the summers. It gets pretty hot around here. The buildings block all the breezes.

But then they turned the water off to save money. I guess they figured they were already spending too much on the people of the projects. So now the fountain is just a big concrete bowl where people gather day and night. It's full of needles, bottles, crack pipes, and all kinds of other nasty stuff. And sitting around the edges are a bunch of young men who by this time next year are going to be either six feet underground or behind bars.

A single woman would be out of her mind to walk into this scene on her own. As recently as last week, I would have been too scared to do it. But I have a new purpose now. I need to find LeVon.

So I hang back by the street for a little while, looking for a tall young man among the seven or eight who are hanging out by the fountain's edge. Every once in a while some crackhead comes stumbling up and has a conversation with one of them. Then there is a whistle, and a little kid comes running out of one of the buildings with a bag in his hand. The dealer gives it to the crackhead. The crackhead gives the dealer cash. The dealer gives the cash to the kid. The kid runs back into the building with it, where he probably sticks it under a bed or something. This is how they make sure they have nothing on them if they get busted.

So they have children running drugs for them. Great. Just my kind of people.

LeVon is not too hard to spot. He stands about six inches above his fellow dealers. And the similarity to Terrell is obvious.

What's weird is that he looks a lot like Dre too. He's got the same slope to his shoulders and the same loose way of moving.

And there's something else about LeVon that surprises me. I see it as I start heading in his direction. I don't want to believe it at first. I think my eyes are playing tricks on me. But as I get closer, I can see it really is him.

LeVon is the one who mugged me last year. Right in front of my own house.

When I realize this, I don't know if I can go on. The terror I felt that day washes over me in a cold wave.

It was broad daylight, about three o'clock in the afternoon. I never saw him coming. I was unloading a bag of groceries from my car. When I closed the door and turned around, there he was. His knife was already in his hand. He was wearing a hat pulled down low. He held the knife casually, like he wouldn't think twice about using it.

"Gimme it," he said.

I knew what he wanted. I dropped my groceries and went for my wallet. He tried to grab the whole thing, but I backed up, shaking my head.

"No," I said. "Please. Just take my cash. Here."

I was so scared my hands were shaking. But I got my money out and handed it over. He looked me up and down, like he was trying to decide what else to take. That's what really chilled me. The way he looked at me—like I wasn't even a person.

Then he was gone.

I didn't even bother calling the police. No point. They're not there to protect poor people from each other. They're there to keep the poor away from the rich.

So here I am, walking toward this person now. The guys on the fountain are just sitting there, waiting for something to happen. When they see me, they elbow each other. I go straight up to him.

"LeVon?" I say.

He looks at me. Then he stands up. I don't think he recognizes me.

"What up?" he says.

"Are you LeVon?" I ask.

"Who the hell are you?" he says. "What you want?"

The terror of that moment comes back to me again. I remember how afraid I was that he was going to hurt me. I wasn't worried for myself. All I could think about was Marco and Dre. I couldn't leave them alone in this life. They had it hard enough already. They were all I thought about then, and they're all I think about now.

I lose my nerve. This whole thing is a mistake. Why did I think this would work? I can't just approach a total stranger and ask him for a kidney. It's insane. I'm an idiot.

I turn and start to walk away, fast.

But I should have known I couldn't get away that easy. I can hear his footsteps behind me.

"Hey!" he says. "Who are you? You better start talking right now!"

And suddenly he's in front of me. I realize there's no walking away from this one. I'm in this far. I have to finish what I started now.

It's not for me, I remind myself. It's for Dre.

I take a deep breath and look him in the eye.

CHAPTER EIGHT

"I have a son named Dre, a couple of years younger than you," I say.

"Yeah? So what?" he says. He's reaching into his pocket. I know his knife is in there. Or maybe he carries a gun now. I need to talk fast.

"Dre's father is Terrell," I say. "Same as your father. Dre is your half brother."

He stops going for his pocket.

"So? I probably got lots of brothers. Papa was a rolling stone, you know?" He looks almost proud. I wonder how he can be proud of his father for abandoning him. Then I wonder if LeVon himself has any kids yet. I wouldn't be at all surprised. People like him think it's funny to knock a girl up and then take off.

"Well, I used to know Terrell a long time ago," I say. "And I just got back from seeing him in prison."

"Yeah? You one of Terrell's hoochies, is that it?"

I want to slap him for that. But instead I just shake my head.

"I haven't been involved with Terrell for a long time," I say. "He left me high and dry. Same way he left your mama."

"Hmm." LeVon doesn't respond to that. "So what you want? Why you come by here? You a cop?"

"No, I'm not a cop. I'm kind of like a nurse. But that's not why I'm here. I just wanted to know if you wanted to meet your brother sometime."

"Why would I wanna do that?" LeVon says.

The truth is, I have no idea. This whole thing seems crazier than ever. All I want now is to get out of here and go home. Dre and I will figure something else out. Maybe if we pray hard enough a donor will appear. Or some other kind of miracle will happen. I must have been nuts for thinking this two-bit thug was going to help me. Look at him. He can't even help himself. Soon enough, he's going to be dead. That's what happens to all these punks. And I hate to say it, but part of me believes that the world is a better place without them. If only there weren't so many more just waiting to take their place.

But I also feel kind of sorry for LeVon. He looks enough like Dre that he brings out the mama in me.

I think about how he must have felt when he was a little boy. He had it even worse than Dre. Not only was his daddy gone, his mama was probably already a drunk back then. I could imagine it all. Neglected for the first years of his life. Going without regular meals because there was no one to cook for him. Being left alone for hours at a time. Scared to death. Never going to school, or if he did, it was just for the hot lunch. Finally ending up on the street, where at least there were other human beings to connect with. Getting taken up into some gang or other. Finding a home. Feeling like at last he belonged somewhere. Learning how to take what he needed from the world. Getting good at it. Not worrying about getting arrested, because he knew as many people in prison as out.

There are thousands of kids like LeVon in this city. Millions in the whole country. It's not right. Not right at all.

"What's your favorite home-cooked meal?" I ask LeVon.

See, I know how to get through to a boy. Sometimes it's just all about the food.

"Why you wanna know that?" he says.

"Because I was thinking you could come over for dinner sometime. Meet Dre. And my other son, Marco. He's just six. You all might like getting to know each other. And we could share a nice meal."

LeVon stares at me like I'm an alien from another planet.

"So, what's your favorite thing to eat?" I ask.

He gives me a funny half smile. And just like that, I'm not afraid of him anymore.

"Roasted chicken and grits with gravy," he says.

"Yeah? Well, you come by sometime, I just might make that for you. If you give me enough notice."

"Yeah, but why?"

"Just because. Why does there have to be a reason?" I feel like a big liar. "It's not right, you guys living so close and not even knowing each other. You could hang out. Become friends."

"Lady, I don't know who you is, but you crazy," he says. He doesn't sound mad anymore. He sounds entertained.

"Here, LeVon," I say. I take a piece of paper and a pen out of my purse and write down my address for him. Now I know I'm crazy. This is a horrible idea. At least I don't have anything worth stealing. "You come by here sometime. We'll have us a real nice dinner. We can hang out, eat, you can play Xbox with the boys. It'll be fun."

LeVon is practically laughing now. It's like I just told him the best joke in the world.

"Sure, okay, lady," he says. "Sounds great." He rolls his eyes.

"Just do me one favor," I say, looking at the other guys sitting around the fountain. "Keep that address to yourself. This is just for you. I don't need every scumbag in the city showing up. Understand?"

LeVon looks surprised. Maybe I shouldn't have called his friends scumbags. But I forgot to be afraid of him, and my real self shone through for a moment. That's what surprised him. He sees I'm not just another cowering victim.

At least, I hope he does.

CHAPTER NINE

"You did *what?*"

Ernest's voice goes so high I think he's going to crack a window. We're in my bedroom, talking. It's the first time he's been in here since we split up, and it's going to be the last too. Ernest has been watching Dre and Marco for me. I brought him in here to tell him what just happened with LeVon. I don't want the boys to hear.

"I had to," I say. "I had to reach out to him. I can't ask him over and then not tell him where I live. He'll come when he's ready."

"Yeah, but Linda," says Ernest, "if this guy is as dangerous as you say he is, you just invited him to break in and rob you."

Ernest doesn't even know that LeVon has already robbed me once. I wonder what he would say to that.

"There's nothing to rob!" I yell. I wave my arms around the room. "Take a look. What do you see? I got a clock radio. Some clothes. A picture of Jesus on the wall. Go out in the living room. I got an old television and an Xbox. That damn Xbox is the most valuable thing I own. It's worth more than my car! And he can have that. Maybe then the boys will spend more time on homework."

"What if he breaks in anyway?" says Ernest. "Then what do you do?"

"I guess I gotta worry about that when it happens," I say.

"Look," says Ernest. "I'm willing to help you through this. I said I would and I mean it. But you gotta check with me first before you do things like this. You're just making things worse."

"I don't have to check with you about anything. Besides, I told you, Ernest. LeVon is probably the only person in the city who can help Dre. Maybe the only person in the whole world, for all I know. I got no other choice. I just need to get through to him."

Ernest can see I'm starting to get upset. The thought of losing Dre is killing me.

"Yeah, I know," he says. "I understand. But listen. You gotta let me stay here tonight."

"*What*? Uh-uh. No way."

"What if he comes here at two in the morning, trying to get in?" Ernest says.

"Ernest, you're the one who's always trying to get in," I say. "You're always looking for some way to get back together with me."

He looks sheepish.

"So?" he says. "Can you blame me?"

Well, he's got a point there. We never want anything as bad as the thing we had and didn't appreciate.

"I wouldn't mind so much if you weren't the one who left in the first place!" I say.

"That's not true," he says. "You threw me out!"

"I had no choice!" I say. "She was calling the house ten times a day! I got my self-respect, you know! I told you, I can put up with a lot, but not with that!"

"Baby, not a day goes by I don't wish I could take it all back," he says.

"Why did you do it anyway? Was I so boring? Were you sick of me?"

"No, no," he says. "I'm just...weak. She came onto me. I couldn't help myself. It's not like I was looking for it. You gotta believe me. I was faithful to you, Linda. But when a woman throws herself at a guy like that..." He shakes his head. "It's pretty hard to say no. It's just the way we're wired."

"That's the dumbest excuse ever," I say. "You have a brain, don't you?"

"Yeah, well, sometimes the big brain gets overruled by the little brain."

"I don't wanna go through all this again," I say. "I've moved on. If it wasn't for Marco, you wouldn't be in my life at all. So just remember that."

"All right," says Ernest humbly.

I look at the window. It's got bars over it, but I imagine a pair of hands ripping them off, the glass shattering, someone climbing in. Someone like LeVon or one of his shady friends. I have to hope he didn't talk about me to any of them.

It would be good to have a man in the house for a night or two. Just to set my mind at ease.

"You can sleep on the couch," I say.

It's ridiculous how grateful he looks. He really must be lonely, I think. After that little escapade with what's-her-name didn't work out, he's been hanging around here like a seagull at a beach picnic. Just hoping for a few scraps of affection to be thrown his way.

"Okay," he says. "Thanks."

"What are you thanking me for? You're supposed to be protecting us."

"Right. And I will."

"But I'm warning you, I'm sleeping with a frying pan," I say. "And if you try anything, I'm going to crack your dome like an egg."

"Come on," says Ernest, looking offended. "What kind of guy do you think I am?"

* * *

Late that night, I lie in bed, looking up at the ceiling. Every little sound I hear gets magnified. Cars go by outside all night long. That's nothing unusual. I can hear Marco snoring in the room he shares with Dre.

Both of them are sleeping peacefully for once. Marco has been having nightmares lately. I tried to spare him the worst, but he's overheard my phone conversations with the doctor. He knows Dre is sick and needs a new kidney. You can't slip anything past that kid.

And Dre is changing before my eyes. He's no kid anymore. This illness has altered him. We don't talk about it, but I know he's fearing the worst. I try to keep things light around here. It's just hard to pretend like there's nothing wrong. And he hates the shunt that's still in his arm, up in his shirt sleeve. He says it makes him feel like a robot.

All I want is what any mother wants. I want my kids to be safe. I want them to have a decent shot at a good life for themselves. I don't want any special favors from the world. But I know from experience that the world is not a fair place.

When I start feeling sorry for myself sometimes, I can get to feeling like we've had more than our fair share of knocks. Thinking that way is a trap. I try to stay clear of it. But late at night, when I'm trying to get to sleep, that's when the bad thoughts close in on me. I feel like I'm surrounded by tigers, just waiting to tear me apart.

Single moms don't get a lot of sleep. I try to tell myself that just this once I can let go and let Ernest do the worrying.

Sometime in the early morning, when the sun is already beginning to color the sky, I finally drift off.

CHAPTER TEN

Dialysis is no big deal. You sit there while your blood runs through a machine and the toxins are taken out. The only bad thing is, it takes a long time. Between three and five hours. So you've got all that time to sit there and wonder about all kinds of bad things.

My mama used to say that a person should always be either working or sleeping, never just sitting still. It's when you're doing nothing that you start to fall apart, little by little. I never believed her before. I never had time to sit still. But now

I see what she means. She had plenty to worry about, my mama. Cancer took my dad twenty years ago. That's when I started to run wild. She fretted over me until cancer took her too, ten years later.

Dre wants me to leave him at the clinic and come back for him. But there's no way I'm leaving him alone. Maybe I should stop treating him like a baby. But this is no time for heroics. I stick it out with him.

"How do you feel?" I ask when it's all done.

"Mama, it's amazing," he said. "I feel great. I feel normal. Like I could go back to school."

"No way," I say. "Too many germs. You're staying home."

"No fair," he grumbles. "I'm going crazy just sitting around."

We get back in the car and head home. He's mad at me now, but in a couple of days he's going to be feeling pretty sick again, and he'll see what I mean. He can't push his luck. Sometimes your luck pushes back.

We're on the street, not far from the projects, when I see a familiar face on the sidewalk. It's LeVon.

Part of me wants to drive on and pretend he's not there. He hasn't spotted me. But another part of me won't let that happen. And that's the part that takes over. I pull up to the curb so he will pass right by us.

"What are you doing, Mama?" Dre asks, confused.

"Yo, LeVon!" I say through the open window. "LeVon! Over here!"

"What are you talking to that guy for?" Dre asks. "He's a dealer!"

"Hold on," I say. "I just need to talk to him a second."

LeVon stops and approaches the car, but he stays back several feet.

"Yeah?" he says. "You wanna partay, hit the boys at the fountain. Don't be doggin' me on the street."

"LeVon, it's Linda, remember?" I say. "I was talking to you the other day."

"Oh, yeah, right," says LeVon. "The crazy lady."

"I wanted to introduce you to somebody. This is Dre. Dre, LeVon is Terrell's son from a lady named Angelique. You guys are brothers. Got the same father anyway."

Dre and LeVon size each other up. I can tell what they think of each other. Dre thinks LeVon is a worthless gang-banger, because that's the way I raised him to think. And LeVon thinks Dre is a weak-ass half-breed whose mama drives him around town in a crappy old car. But the word *brother* hangs in the air like a cloud of smoke. And neither of them is the first to wave it away.

"S'up," says LeVon.

"Hey," says Dre.

"You remember about that dinner?" I say. "Why don't you come on over tonight?"

Dre looks at me like I've lost my mind.

LeVon just shakes his head.

"This is all very touching, but I got places to be," he says. "We can have our little reunion some other time."

"All right," I say reluctantly. I don't want to push my luck. Because sometimes your luck pushes back.

LeVon and I see the cop car at the same time. I can hear dealers whistling warnings to each other. The cop car rolls slowly down the block, like a shark cruising for swimmers. LeVon freezes up.

"On second thought," he says, "maybe I will come right now."

"Get in," I say.

LeVon gets in the backseat and slams the door.

"I can't believe this," says Dre, putting his face in his hands.

"Go ahead. Roll," says LeVon.

"Wait," I say. "You're not holding, are you?"

"Damn, lady, what you think? Of course I'm holding," says LeVon. The cop rolls past, and LeVon sinks down out of sight. "I'm a drug dealer. That's what drug dealers do. You think I wanna be seen in this here splendid automobile because it got style?"

"Pass it off," I say. "Get rid of it."

I don't have much room to boss LeVon around right now. I need him on my side too bad. But I have a strict rule about drugs: keep them the hell away from my kids. No exceptions.

"Go ahead," I say. "Do it."

LeVon rolls his eyes. For a minute I think he's just going to get out of the car. Only the cop is keeping him from doing that. But then he whistles out the window, and another kid comes running up. LeVon takes a paper bag out of his jacket and hands it to the kid.

"Stash that and be quick," he says. "And I'm gonna count it, yo. Every single one better be there when I get back."

The kid takes the bag and disappears.

"I hope you happy now," says LeVon. He looks out the rear window. The cop has stopped about fifty feet away. I can't tell if we've attracted his attention or not. I start moving.

"You take that stuff, or you just sell it, LeVon?" I ask him.

LeVon laughs.

"Hell, no," he says. "I don't touch that stuff. It's for suckers. I'm a businessman. I got a plan. I'm gonna retire in a few years. Sit back and live large."

"Yeah? You ever think about doing something else with your life? Like doing something noble?"

"Something *what*?" says LeVon.

"Something *what*?" says Dre at the same time.

"Noble," I say. "You know. Selfless. Something to help other people, instead of just yourself. Like your mother, maybe. She's alone and she's got no one to take care of her."

LeVon laughs again. It's a loud, unpleasant bark.

"My mama too wasted to care right now whether she's alone or not," he says. "That's the way it always was. She didn't take care of me. So why would I take care of her? Besides, it's too late for me. I'm on the path."

"You're only nineteen years old," I say.

"Nineteen in the projects is like ninety in the rest of the world," says LeVon. "Damn, lady, don't you know anything at all?"

CHAPTER ELEVEN

This has to be the most awkward car ride in the history of car rides. I feel sorry for Dre. I've never said a word to him about LeVon. He doesn't even know I went to see Terrell. I can tell by the way he's looking at me that I have a lot of explaining to do.

I'll tell you later, Dre, I think.

But I'm going to use this chance all I can. I just happen to have a chicken in the fridge and a box of grits in the cupboard. I can make LeVon some dinner and get him to hang for a while. Maybe play some

Xbox with the boys. That will chill him out. It's the first step.

Ernest is at my place again, watching Marco. He could just take him back to his place, but he likes hanging out in the house we used to share. The look on his face when the three of us walk through the door is priceless.

I introduce LeVon to Ernest and then to Marco.

"You can think of Marco as your brother too, if you want," I tell LeVon.

Something in LeVon changes when he meets the little guy. His expression gets softer. I think he likes the idea of having a younger brother.

I take Ernest in the back room and tell him to go home. He wants to fight about it, but now is not the time.

"This is too delicate," I say. "I don't need you and your attitude messing it up."

"What attitude?" he says.

"The attitude you're showing me right now. And you're giving LeVon dirty looks. I know he's a banger, but we gotta give him a chance."

"Oh, sure," says Ernest. "I'm good enough when you need someone to watch Marco or to keep you safe. But as soon as you don't need me anymore, you kick me out. I'm not your servant, Linda. You better think about the way you're acting."

He's right. I have been using him lately. It's not fair. But I'm not doing it for me.

"It's all about Dre," I say. "That's really all I'm thinking about right now. But maybe when all this is over, you and I can talk."

"Really?" Ernest brightens.

"Don't go reading anything into that," I say. "I said talk. I didn't say get back together."

He nods happily. "Okay," he says. I can tell he thinks we're getting back together anyway. I'll have to straighten him out later. But for now he goes home with no more argument.

I pop the chicken in the oven. In the living room, the boys have fired up the Xbox. Marco is teaching LeVon how to steal cars on *Grand Theft Auto IV*. I hate that game, but they begged me so hard to let them buy it that I gave in. I don't even say a word to them now. I just let them bond over what boys like best, which seems to be violent, mindless entertainment. I can hear Marco's digital camera go off too. He must be taking pictures. He loves to take pictures of just about everything he can, including LeVon, I guess.

When dinner is ready, we all sit down at the tiny table. Marco and Dre bow their heads automatically. LeVon looks at them, confused.

"Thank you, Lord, for another day," I say. "And thank you for this meal."

"And thank you for our new brother LeVon," says Marco. "And thank you for letting LeVon give Dre a new kidney. Amen."

Uh-oh.

There's a long silence. Marco must have overheard more than I realized. Dammit, Marco, I think. Can't slip anything past that kid.

"Thank you for giving Dre a new *what?*" LeVon says.

"Kidney!" says Marco happily.

LeVon puts down his knife and fork.

"What he talkin' about?" he asks me.

"I…" I'm speechless. "I, uh—"

"What you need a new kidney for?" LeVon asks Dre.

Dre looks blameless, but then he didn't know any of this business about matching blood types or any of that. I kept it all from him. I made sure he couldn't hear whenever I talked to the doctor. Too bad I didn't do the same with Marco.

"I've got renal failure," he says. "I get dialysis. So I need a new kidney, or I'm gonna die."

"You're not gonna die," I say quickly.

"That's not what the doctor said," says Dre.

"Yeah, but what's Marco mean, LeVon giving Dre a kidney?" LeVon says. "'Cause LeVon ain't giving away no kidneys."

I could play this one of two ways. I could say Marco was just talking nonsense, making up crazy stories the way little kids do. Or I could tell him the truth. I always try to tell the truth, even when it's not pretty. I feel like in the long run it's the best way.

So I tell LeVon the truth: Dre needs one of his kidneys to live.

LeVon stands up. He's so mad he's shaking.

"This is sick!" he says. "I feel like I'm in one of them horror movies or something! You just wanted my *kidney*? You people is crazy, you know that? Damn! Get me outta here before y'all try to eat me or something!"

Marco is staring at LeVon. Dre is staring at me. LeVon is heading for the door. And I'm sitting with my face in my hands. Because I feel like I have royally screwed up.

"LeVon," I say. "I'm really sorry."

"Sorry my ass!" LeVon yells. "Stay the hell away from me, lady! Jesus! I had people come after my stash, and I had people come after my money. But ain't nobody ever come after one of my kidneys before!"

He slams the door. I can hear him still yelling all the way down the sidewalk.

My boys are quiet for a moment. Then Marco picks up his drumstick and starts eating his dinner as though nothing has happened.

"Don't be mad at me," I say to Dre. He's looking at me like he's disgusted.

"That was uncool," he says. "You invited him over just to get his kidney? Damn, Mom. That's messed up."

"It wasn't like that," I say, but the truth is, it was like that.

CHAPTER TWELVE

A month goes by. Then another month. Then a third. Time has slowed down to the speed of an ant walking through syrup. It's just work, dialysis, wait. Work, dialysis, wait. I take Dre for treatment three times a week. That's twelve or fifteen hours of sitting and watching his blood run through this machine. Dre hates dialysis. He hates not going to school. He hates everything about his life right now.

I can understand that. I'm not too happy myself. I've been worried about money for so long now that if I won the lottery tomorrow, I would keep worrying just out of habit.

Every time the phone rings I jump a mile. I'm hoping it's Dr. Wendell, calling to say they found a donor. But it never is.

Miss Emily, my client, dies. I'm there with her, holding her hand, when she passes. It's a beautiful moment. She had a long life. It's not tragic when someone as old as her goes. It's just natural.

I get a new client. Mr. Varner is fifty and recovering from spinal surgery. He's grumpy and obnoxious, and he doesn't like people of color. Every time I go to his house he tells me he's going to check to make sure I didn't steal anything. Needless to say, I don't read to him from Barack Obama's book. I don't read to him at all. I go to work and do my job without thinking about it. Sometimes that's how it is.

But these hours don't cut it. I got the skills, but I can't pay the bills. So I keep looking for more work. No one else is hiring. I could get a minimum-wage job, but by the time I was done paying someone to look after the boys I would be deeper in the hole. This is why people go on welfare. The system makes it so you can't afford to work.

I have no choice. I go back to the welfare office. I tell myself it's not my fault. It's the economy. After all, I would crawl on my hands and knees over piles of razor blades to help my kids. I'm lucky all I have to do is fill out some forms. And put up with a lot of insulting questions. And surrender my dignity at the door. That's all there is to it. I'm not one of those who expects a free ride. It's not my fault there's no jobs.

Then one day, the phone does ring. It's not Dr. Wendell or the hospital. It's LeVon. I can hardly believe it.

"Where are you?" I ask.

"I'm in the joint," he says. "Been here a little while. I caught a case after I saw you. Got locked up. We need to talk."

If LeVon wants me to help him somehow, I will. I feel like it's the least I could do to make things right. I never felt okay about what happened. He got the wrong idea, but still.

So I go back to the prison, the same one where I last saw Terrell. I meet LeVon in the same waiting room. Once again I think about how much he looks like his father. And like Dre.

"What happened, LeVon?" I ask. "How'd you end up here?"

"Aw, somebody got shot over some drugs," he says. "I didn't have nothing to do with it. But they trying to pin it on me. Looks like it's gonna work too. I'm gonna be here a while."

"Sorry to hear it."

He shrugs. He has no expectations from his life. He takes what he's given and he rolls with it.

"Listen," I say, "about what happened. I was never gonna come right out and ask you to give Dre a kidney. It wasn't like that. I really did want you guys to get to know each other. Once you knew what was up, if you decided you could help him out, great. If not, we would understand. Nobody would ever hold a gun to your head about it. You know what I mean? We're not that way. I just didn't know what else to do."

He nods.

"Yeah, I feel you," he says. "It was just a little weird, you know? Anyway, I had plenty of time to think about all that. Some stuff has happened, yo."

"Like what?"

"Terrell, he's dead. He got stabbed."

LeVon's face is so flat when he tells me this that he might as well be talking about the weather.

"LeVon, I'm so sorry," I say. "I had no idea."

He shrugs.

"Ain't nothin' but a thing," he says. "He wasn't nothin' to me. We hardly even talked to each other. I guess someone had a beef. That happens in the joint. Anyway, it got me thinking. What you said in the car. About doing something noble."

I can't believe he actually remembers that. Hope begins to well up inside me. But I can't say a word. I just have to listen.

"And there was something else. I feel like I owe you one. I don't know if you knew me or not when you saw me the first time. But when you came up to me at the Fountain, I was, like, Uh-oh. There's that lady I done robbed a while ago."

"So you did remember me."

LeVon nods.

"And I just wanted to say, that wasn't right," he says. "It was nothing personal. I had some numbers I needed to make up. Just business, you know?"

"You scared the hell out of me," I say. "I thought I was gonna die."

He nods again.

"Yeah, I'm sorry about that," he says. "I'm trying to put things right in my life. Trying to turn things around. I don't wanna die in this place like old Terrell did. So I kinda feel like I owe you one. I'm looking at a long time here. Maybe we can help each other out. You feel me?"

"You mean…"

"Dre can have it," LeVon says. "He's my brother anyway. I never had a brother to do for me. I can live with one kidney, right?"

"Right," I say. "You could have a totally normal life. And so could he."

"Maybe it would get me outta here early too," says LeVon.

"Maybe it would," I say. "I can talk to the parole board. Tell them how you've helped us. Let them see what kind of a person you really are."

"Yeah," says LeVon. "So let's do this thing. Go ahead. Call who you gotta call. Let them know they can come get me whenever they want. I ain't goin' nowhere."

I take LeVon's hands and squeeze them.

"No touching!" yells a guard from across the room.

"Thank you," I whisper. "You're noble, all right. You're the most noble man who ever lived."

CHAPTER THIRTEEN

There are tests that have to be done before we can be sure LeVon is a good match. These are the same tests Terrell failed. But LeVon passes them with flying colors. The drug question was an easy one, he says. He's never shot up in his life. He only sold it. He never touched the stuff.

So it's a go. There's nothing stopping us now. Dre is going to get his kidney.

LeVon has been told by the parole judge that he'll get a break on his sentence if he goes through with the donation. Seems they have some kind of special law about that.

Besides, one of the witnesses who helped put him away is changing his story.

And it helps that I'm putting in a good word for him. I've told the judge that LeVon won't be going back out on the street when he's released. He can come and live with us if he wants to. He's not a kid anymore. He doesn't need anyone to take care of him. But everyone needs some-place to go.

LeVon has decided he wants out of the game. I guess seeing your father die in prison will do that. He wants to turn his life around somehow. He seems more scared about that than about the operation. Change is a scary thing.

The day of the surgery, they prep LeVon and Dre together. They have a few minutes to talk, lying side by side in their hospital beds.

"I just wanted to say thanks," Dre says. "You know I appreciate it."

"Yeah, I know," says LeVon. "Man, I feel like I'm on vacation. Even a hospital is better than the joint."

"What's it like in there?" asks Dre.

"You don't wanna know," says LeVon. "Crazy. It's never quiet. Never safe. You got to watch your back every minute. People be screaming, crying, fighting, yelling, begging, all kinds of crazy stuff. Man can't hear himself think. It just goes on and on."

"People be gettin' killed too," says Dre quietly.

"Yeah," says LeVon. "There is that."

They are both reflective for a moment. Dre knows about Terrell. I made sure I told him right away. I don't believe in keeping things like that from my boys. They have a right to know what kind of world they're living in. And Dre has a right to know what happened to his own father.

"Anyway," says LeVon, "you get yourself right again, you got to do somethin' with yourself. Not just sit around playin' Xbox all day long. You feel me? Take my kidney and make it work for you. Use it to do somethin' good."

"Something noble," says Dre, grinning at me.

"Yo, noble lady," says LeVon, "you bring me any chicken? I never did get to finish my dinner."

"After you get out, I'll make you all the roasted chickens you want," I say.

"Yeah, that sounds good," says LeVon. "Roasted chickens day and night. I can hardly wait."

"What are you gonna do with yourself?" Dre asks LeVon. "When all this is over, and you get back out?"

LeVon shrugs. I can tell it's bugging him he doesn't have an answer for this yet.

"I dunno," he says. "I been in the game a long time. Hard to imagine what all I might do if not that."

"You finish high school?" Dre asks.

"Hell, no. You kidding me? I stopped going to school when I was nine."

"Nine?" Dre is in shock. "You been working that long?"

"Yeah, that's the way it was," says LeVon. "I had to eat somehow. I wanna go straight, I'm gonna have to go back to school first. And that's gonna be hard."

"Worry about one thing at a time," I suggest. "Today is a big day. You don't have to solve everything all at once."

Dr. Wendell comes in. He's wearing surgical scrubs.

"How you guys doing?" he asks. "Ready to get going?"

"Ready as I'm gonna be," says Dre.

"Me too," says LeVon. "Let's do it."

"You're both going to be fine," says Dr. Wendell. "When you wake up you're going to have sore throats and sore incisions. But you'll be up and around in no time.

You're young and healthy. You have long lives ahead of you."

It's true, I think. A month ago, you could not have said that about either of them. Now, thanks to what one is doing for the other, they both have a second shot.

A nurse comes in and puts a needle in LeVon's arm. They will use this to put him to sleep. They don't have to put one in Dre's because he already has one.

"All right," says Dr. Wendell to me. "We're going to take them now. You can wait in the reading room if you want. We'll call you when they're out."

I hug and kiss my boy. Then I hug and kiss LeVon too. He acts embarrassed, but I can tell he likes it. I wonder when the last time was that he got kissed by his mother. She doesn't even know what he's doing today. I asked LeVon if he wanted to tell her, but he said no. She's tucked into a bottle somewhere, dreaming her life away.

Maybe she's even dead by now herself. LeVon doesn't know and he doesn't care. I can't understand how a mother could abandon her own son the way she did.

"I'll see you boys in a little while," I say. "I'll be praying for you."

"Okay, Mama," says Dre. "Here we go."

"See you, Linda," says LeVon.

The nurses wheel their beds out of the room and down the hall. I skip the reading room and go straight to the chapel. This is where I'll spend the next few hours, until they come get me. On my knees. Praying as hard as I know how.

CHAPTER FOURTEEN

These days, getting over an operation doesn't seem to take as long as it used to. I remember when I was a kid, they would keep you for a whole week if you had your tonsils out. Now they can remove a breast and send you home the same day. Not for a kidney transplant though. They want to keep both these boys in for three or four days, just to make sure everything went all right. And that won't be the end of it either. They will need regular checkups. They have certain restrictions. But they can lead full lives.

The first day seems to go fine. They come out of surgery and wake up a little bit later. Both of them are groggy. Both of them are in pain. That's normal. They sleep a lot. That's normal too.

The next day Dre gets up and tries walking around. He does fine. He complains he's sore. There's a drainage tube in the incision that's bothering him. But that will come out in a few days.

LeVon is not feeling so great. He says he feels hot all over. The nurse takes his temperature. He's got a fever. That's not terribly unusual, she says, but she looks worried. She calls the doctor.

Dr. Wendell comes right away. He orders stronger antibiotics for LeVon. He's got an infection, he says. This is fairly common. It's not good, but it doesn't have to be bad news either. If they keep an eye on it and treat it with drugs, it should go away.

It doesn't.

"Man, what's wrong with me?" says LeVon the next day. "I feel horrible." He's got a high fever now. He says he's cold all the time. But he's sweating.

"This happens every once in a while," says Dr. Wendell. "It's not the end of the world. Don't worry. We can treat it. We'll give you stronger antibiotics. It should go away very soon."

But it doesn't.

"This is not good," Dr. Wendell says to me in private. It's day three after the operation. Dre is doing great and is almost ready to leave. They're not allowing him in the same room as LeVon. This bothers him a lot. He wants to thank his brother in person. He wants to be with him while he gets better. But they won't let him, because they don't want him to get sick. His system is still too vulnerable.

"What's happening?" I say.

"It's a superbug," says Dr. Wendell. "They've been cropping up lately. The germs that cause infections are evolving to fight the drugs we use. They're getting stronger and tougher. This is one of those new kinds of bacteria. It's winning the fight."

"So what's going to happen?"

"We're not giving up," says Dr. Wendell. "Not by a long shot. But I can't give him any more antibiotics. We don't have anything stronger. I'm doing everything I can for him. We have to trust that because he's young and healthy, he'll pull through."

A little later I go into LeVon's room. He's not awake and he's not asleep. He stares at the ceiling, his eyes half closed. His breathing is shallow. I pull back the sheets and look at his toes. They're starting to curl.

Oh no.

"Listen to me," I say. "It's not supposed to be like this. You're not even twenty years old. You can beat this thing. You can fight it.

You're tough. You made it this far. You beat gangsters and drug dealers and life on the street. You mean to tell me a little old bug is gonna get you? Come on. Get real. Get your ass up out of this bed right now."

LeVon doesn't answer. A nurse comes in. She and I look at each other. Nurses see it all. They are very practical people. And I can tell by the look in her eyes what this lady is thinking: Pretty soon this room is gonna have a free bed in it.

"How is he doing?" Dre asks me later, when I'm back in his room.

"He's not doing so good," I say.

"What? Are you serious? I can't believe this."

"I know. It wasn't supposed to be this way."

"Won't they let me see him?"

"Baby, if you pick up what he has, it could kill you. That's the plain truth. So you stay away from him. I'm sorry. I know you want nothing more than to see him right now. But it ain't gonna happen."

There is no one else to be with LeVon as he lies in his bed, waiting to get better or not. He has no one else who cares. If it wasn't for me, he'd be alone. So I sit there with him, holding his hand and talking to him.

"You know, you changed a lot of lives with what you did," I say. "This is one of the greatest things a person can do for another person. Whatever wrong you think you might have done in your life, this takes care of it. You're even. You're clean. You can hold your head high."

He doesn't answer. His hand is dry and cool.

I'm sitting with him just like this when he passes. It's three o'clock in the morning.

My practical side takes over. I call the nurse. She comes in and begins to try to revive him. It doesn't work. The doctor on duty comes rushing in and does the same. There is nothing they can do. They pronounce him dead a little before four AM.

Dre is asleep down the hall. I'll tell him in the morning. No need to wake him now.

Suddenly I don't know what to do with myself. So I go into the bathroom and lock the door. And I cry for LeVon, and all the LeVons of the world. The ones who never had a chance to begin with.

CHAPTER FIFTEEN

I t's over a year later. The date is September 1. It's morning. Dre is getting ready for school. After a long delay, he's about to start his senior year, and he's never been more excited.

"Mom! Have you seen my tie?" he asks for the third time.

"It's on your bed," I tell him, also for the third time.

"Oh yeah, right."

"How come I can't wear a tie?" pouts Marco.

"Because they don't wear ties in first grade," says Dre. "You'd probably get it caught on something and hang yourself."

"Dre! That's terrible," I say.

"Sorry, Mama. But you know it's true." Dre finds his tie and puts it on. I help him straighten it. Just as I finish, a car pulls up.

"My dad's here!" Marco says. He's all excited.

Ernest gets out of the driver's side. Yvonne, his new wife, gets out of the passenger side. She's slow and awkward. Being pregnant will do that to you.

"Hey, buddy!" Ernest says to Marco. "You almost ready to go?"

"Are we gonna take a picture first?" Marco says.

"That's why I'm all dressed up," says Ernest. "I wouldn't miss your first day of big-kid school for anything."

"Hi, Linda, how are you?" says Yvonne.

"I'm fine, Yvonne. You feeling all right?"

"Pretty good. The morning sickness has passed."

"Glad to hear it." I smile. I like Yvonne. After I broke it to Ernest that it would never work for us to get back together, he realized he had to move on. And move on he did. Yvonne was someone he met through work. She's good for him, I can tell. I don't worry that Ernest is going to screw this one up, either. He's learned a lot from his past mistakes. Too bad he didn't figure that out sooner. But none of us is perfect. And I've learned it's important to forgive people. It's the greatest gift you can give yourself.

"Looking good, Dre," says Ernest. "Excited to start your last year of high school?"

"Excited is not the word," says Dre. "I've been waiting for this a long time."

It hasn't been an easy year. There were a couple of health setbacks for Dre. While they were not life-threatening, he did have to miss a whole year of school after his transplant. He had the option to get home-schooled, and that's what we did. But there were some things he couldn't do at home if he wanted to pursue his new goal of becoming a doctor. Not just any doctor—a kidney specialist. My kitchen doesn't make a very good chemistry lab. Besides, he also wanted the experience of going to real classes, of being a normal kid again. He's going to be a year older than everybody else, but that's not a bad thing. A little maturity will serve him well.

We all go inside the house. Marco gets bossy, lining us all up in front of the couch for the picture. Yvonne holds his camera. She has to back up to fit us all in. My house is so small she's practically in the front yard. But finally she's ready.

"Wait!" says Dre. "I almost forgot."

He runs to the door and takes down a picture that hangs there. Then he gets back in the shot and holds the picture up.

It's a shot of LeVon. Marco took it the day he came here. LeVon is looking up at the camera. He doesn't look anything like a gangster. He looks like a big kid sitting on the floor, video game controls in his hand, hat on sideways. He's even got a half smile on his face.

"Okay, now we're all here," says Dre. He holds the picture up in front of him.

"One, two, three!" says Yvonne. She presses the shutter. The flash goes off once, twice, then three times.

"Okay, let's go," says Ernest. He's taking Marco to school. I told him he could have this moment with his little boy. I'm going to have my own moment with Dre. He doesn't know it, but this day is just as big for me as it is for him.

Ernest, Yvonne and Marco leave first. Then it's just Dre and me.

"You ready?" I say.

"Yeah, I'm ready," says Dre. He hangs LeVon's picture up again next to the front door. "Let's go."

Dre grabs his book bag and his jacket. On his way out the door he reaches up and touches the picture. He doesn't say anything. But he does this every time he leaves the house. I know what it means. It means *Thank you.*

LeVon had it rough. He said himself that making it to nineteen in the projects was like making it to ninety in the rest of the world. Sad to say, but for a young black man, that's the truth. He was more likely to end up dead or behind bars than he was to succeed. That's not right. But that's the world we live in, until we choose to change it.

Every time I see that face, I think of the fact that if it wasn't for him, I wouldn't have my son anymore. So I touch LeVon's picture too.

"Thank you for my son," I whisper, quiet enough so Dre doesn't hear. He gets embarrassed by me a lot lately. I don't care though. Sometimes a mother is going to embarrass her children no matter what she does.

Dre is already outside, waiting in the car. He's not just impatient to get to school. He's impatient to begin the rest of his life. He wants to do something noble with it. He's got the fire in him to make that happen. Dre knows he has to live two lives now—his and LeVon's. Nothing is going to slow him down. Nothing is going to stop him.

"You ready?" I ask him.

"Yeah, I'm ready," he says.

"Put your seatbelt on," I say.

"Mama," Dre says, "it's on."

"Sorry," I say. I guess I just can't help myself.

That's how it is when you're a mom. You don't stop being one just because your kid turns eighteen. Motherhood is for life. And I mean that in more ways than one.

ACKNOWLEDGMENTS

My thanks to Dr. Kate Johnson and Dr. John Jenkins for their technical assistance in the editing of this work.

Something Noble is **W I L L I A M KOWALSKI**'s third title in the Rapid Reads series, following on the success of *The Barrio Kings* (2010) and *The Way It Works* (2010). Kowalski is the award-winning author of four previous novels, including the international bestseller *Eddie's Bastard*. He lives on the South Shore of Nova Scotia with his wife and children.

Titles in the Series

RAPID READS